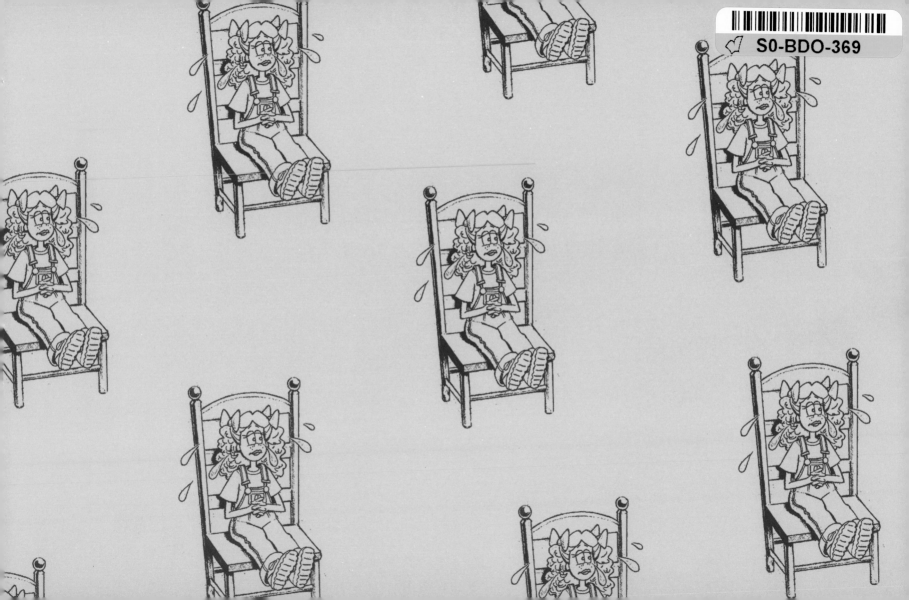

Thanks for believing in me, Grandma!
I love you.

For information regarding permission, write to:
8329 Nieman Rd.• Lenexa,Kansas •66214

Published by Yesteryear Publishing Company
Printed in Hong Kong. All rights reserved.
ISBN 0-97-026790-8
Library of Congress Card Number 00-106128

Willamena came home
from a long day at school.
She threw her books down
and climbed up on a stool.
Her mom kissed her forehead
and brought her a snack,
then poured out fresh strawberries
from a brown paper sack.

She hummed a tune happily
as she hiked up the stairs,
then kissed all her teddy bears
aligned in the chairs.
She laid down near her bed
and kicked her feet way up high.
THAT'S when Willamena started to cry.

She thought,
"How can I be crying?
I'm happy in every way.
I even made an 'A' on
my science test today."

The tears started coming out one after the other, then she yelled loudly downstairs for her mother.

"I can't stop crying, Mom! What's wrong with me? I'm not a sad kid. I really am happy!"

So her mom got a tissue
and then wiped her eyes,
but the tears wouldn't stop
and got

LARGER

IN

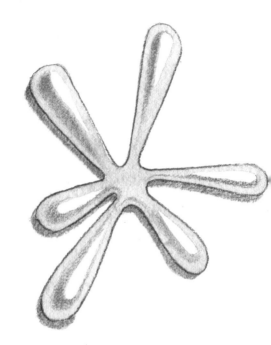

Her mom said,
"There's something strange happening. I'll call your Dad!"
Willamena couldn't believe the endless tears she had.

She tried to stop them from coming out,
but they just kept going...

...on and on her tears
kept flowing !

Puddles of tears added up all over the floor,
then poured out the bedroom door!
Frantically, her mom called everyone she knew
and screamed,

"TEARS ARE FILLING UP MY HOUSE AND I DON'T KNOW WHAT TO DO!!!"

Her older brother told her friends
about the tears and all.

Then called a plumber to rescue her
on an emergency house call!

The plumber checked the leak in her eyes
and was puzzled in despair.

"I just can't fix this enormous leak,"
he said with his one-eyed glare.

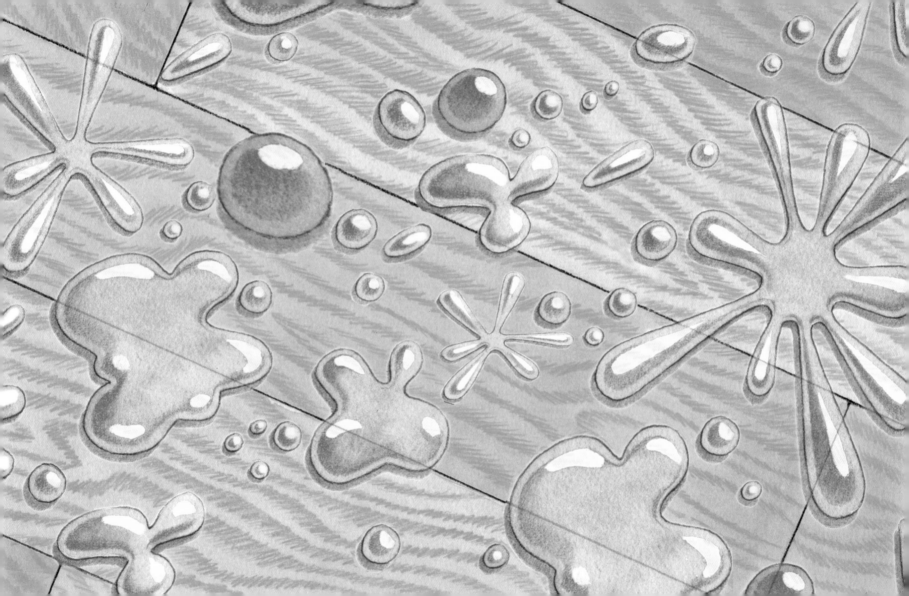

Her mom asked her kindly,
"Will you stop crying
PRETTY PLEASE ???
I'll even get down and beg you
on my hands and knees!"

But STILL...

...Willamena cried!

A funny-looking clown came over
just to make her laugh.
He stretched a shiny red balloon
that made a neat giraffe!
He brought out a fluffy feather
and tickled her bare little toes,
then tried to stop her leaky eyes
by putting on puppet shows!

Willamena's tears kept dripping out
and NOTHING made her stop.
Her mom dashed for lots of towels
and the clown ran for the mop!
Her mom yelled,
"HONEY, STOP YOUR TEARS!
WHAT'S THE MATTER WITH YOU?"
The clown shouted,
"I'M OUT OF TOYS, YA KNOW!
I ONLY BROUGHT A FEW!!!"

Tears rolled down the stairs
and rushed out through the house!
Pretty soon everyone had to swim—
even her pet fish and mouse.
The mouse paddled very quickly
and started heading North.
The fish bowl was going backwards
while swaying back and forth!

Her tears flooded all the streets
and neighbors climbed into their boats.
The kids hurried for their innertubes
and their swimming pool floats!
An old man jumped right off
his neighbor's wooden fence.
Things got out of control
and then got pretty intense!
One guy sat and fished some
in all the millions of tears.
This was the weirdest event
the town had in 100 years!

Willamena's Dad got home.
He was worried from it all!
Then their family dog came in
from playing "Fetch the Ball".
The dog, Jack, swam up the stairs
where Willamena wept.
He held his breath and blew some bubbles—
there was something he had left.

He discovered his ball from way under there.
Then JACK started crying as they all stood with a stare.

"Let me see what's in your mouth!"
Willamena's Dad pointed and said.
"That's not a ball, you silly, Jack!
It's an onion you have instead!"
He asked, "What's an onion doing up here
where it doesn't belong?
Onions need to go in the kitchen!
Am I right or am I wrong?"

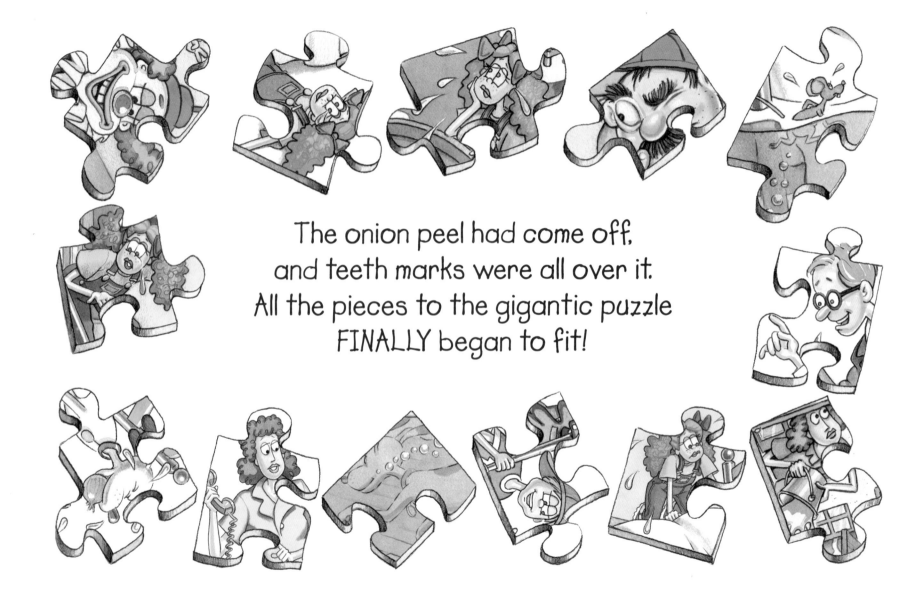

The onion peel had come off,
and teeth marks were all over it.
All the pieces to the gigantic puzzle
FINALLY began to fit!

Willamena said, "One day Jack was in the kitchen
and thought the onion was a toy.
He hid it underneath my bed! I can't believe it! WOW! OH BOY!"

Her Mom said,
"When onions are cut and peeled,
they make people's eyes water,
but usually they aren't cases
like my crying daughter."

They threw the onion away
and all the tears disappeared.
The neighbors threw a party
and they all "YA-HOOED" and cheered.

- And they lived happily ever after -

"Thank you, Mrs. Ozias' Third Grade Class! I had so much fun looking at all your imaginative drawings you drew for me to show your favorite parts of the Willamena story. You helped inspire me to follow my dreams. I hope you follow your dreams, too! THINK BIG!!! The sky is the limit on possibilities. You can do anything you want to do and be anybody that you want to be. Take care and stay safe."- *Lisa*

AUTHOR: *Lisa Cooper*

"I am happily married and a mother of two young daughters, Ashley (11) and Alyssa (9).

I started writing humorous rhythmic rhymes when I was in high school, but never actually set out to get them published. I wrote this story in 1998 and read it to my daughter's 3rd grade class. The enthusiastic response from the students, along with their inspirational giggles, encouraged me to find an artist and publish this story. I also have written six other stories similar to this one that I am currently preparing for printing.

My background is working in the fields of: hair/make-up artistry, promotions, entertainment, and graphic design. I worked along side my wonderful husband, an experienced artist, who helped me with the design of the book.

Together we had a blast! I hope you enjoy this story and find it amusing and funny. Laughter is one thing I truly believe in! It's something David, our kids and I do a lot!"

ILLUSTRATOR: *George Martin*

George Fisher Martin was born in New Jersey in 1947 and grew up on the Jersey shore. He attended the Kansas City Art Institute, receiving a B.F.A with a major in Oil Painting in 1975.

George, a comic at heart, made the characters in this story come to life with his brilliant imagination. Doing what he loves best, he works as a freelance illustrator for book publishers, greeting card companies, toy manufacturers, advertising firms and motion picture productions. He has a passion for painting landscapes and sells his work at various art galleries. He lives happily in a quaint little house tucked away in the woods with his lovely wife, four dogs and a cat.

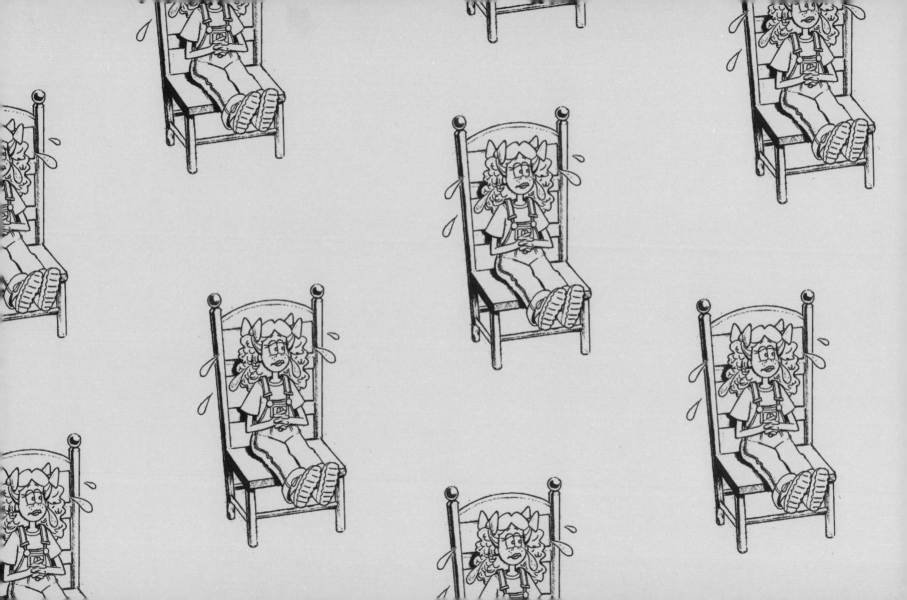